UNICORN ACADEMY

Ariana broke off suddenly. Coming toward them was a long line of rabbits, their tails flashing white as they hopped along. "Where are they going?" she wondered aloud.

Rosa frowned. "They look like they're running away fr̶o̶m̶ ̶t̶h̶e̶ ̶ ̶ ̶ ̶"

LOOK OUT FOR MORE ADVENTURES AT

UNICORN ACADEMY

Sophia and Rainbow

Scarlett and Blaze

Ava and Star

Isabel and Cloud

Layla and Dancer

Olivia and Snowflake

Rosa and Crystal

Ariana and Whisper

★ ★ ★

UNICORN ACADEMY

Ariana and Whisper

JULIE SYKES

illustrated by LUCY TRUMAN

A STEPPING STONE BOOK™

Random House 🏠 New York

Text copyright © 2019 by Julie Sykes and Linda Chapman
Cover art and interior illustrations copyright © 2019 by Lucy Truman

All rights reserved. Published in the United States by Random House Children's Books, a division of Penguin Random House LLC, New York. Originally published in paperback in the United Kingdom by Nosy Crow Ltd, London, in 2019.

Random House and the colophon are registered trademarks and A Stepping Stone Book and the colophon are trademarks of Penguin Random House LLC.

Visit us on the Web! rhcbooks.com

Educators and librarians, for a variety of teaching tools, visit us at RHTeachersLibrarians.com

Library of Congress Cataloging-in-Publication Data is available upon request.
ISBN 978-0-593-17948-2 (trade) — ISBN 978-0-593-17949-9 (lib. bdg.)
ISBN 978-0-593-17950-5 (ebook)

Printed in the United States of America
6
First American Edition

For Antonia,
who is also magic

CHAPTER 1

Ariana woke to the sound of her unicorn alarm clock whinnying good morning. She stretched out a hand and switched it off, then carefully folded back her blue-and-silver blanket and swung her legs out of bed. Her toes sank into something soft, and she frowned. What was that? Leaning over, Ariana saw Matilda's hoodie crumpled on the floor.

"Matilda!" Ariana sighed, looking across at the girl in the next bed. Even in sleep, Matilda somehow managed to make Diamond dorm look messy. Her red hair was spread over her pillow in a sea of tangles, and her blanket hung from the edge of the bed.

As Ariana picked up the hoodie, a large spider with red stripes on its back scuttled across the sleeve. Ariana squealed and flung the hoodie back down, waking Rosa, Freya, and Violet.

"Ariana, are you all right?" said Violet, sitting up quickly.

"What's going on?" demanded Freya.

"Why did you scream?" said Rosa.

Only Matilda was still asleep, snoring softly.

"There's a sp-sp-spider," Ariana stuttered, pointing at the floor where the spider was picking its way over Matilda's hoodie. "I don't like spiders."

"Is that all?" Rosa groaned, flopping back against her pillow.

"Poor spider. It's probably trying to find its way outside," said Violet, pushing her dark braid over her shoulder and going to investigate.

"Let's help it," said Freya, joining her. Gently, she scooped the spider up in her hands. "Aren't the red stripes on its back unusual? I've never seen one like it before. Open the window for me, Ariana."

Ariana stared at Freya in horror. What was she doing picking it up? Red meant danger, didn't it? What if the spider bit her?

"The window, Ariana!" Freya said impatiently.

Ariana hurried to the window and flung it wide open. She shrank back as Freya passed her, just in case the spider tried to escape. "Be careful!"

Freya rolled her eyes. "I can't believe you're scared of spiders. It's not going to hurt us. Surely you know there are no dangerous spiders on Unicorn Island?"

Ariana bit her lip, not wanting to admit she

didn't know much about creepy-crawlies. She just knew she didn't like them!

Freya held the spider as it sent out a thread of silk and sailed down the wall, but before she could close the window, Ariana saw a small emerald-green lizard climbing up the side of Matilda's wardrobe.

"Watch out!" she shrieked.

"Ariana, don't freak out. It's just a harmless lizard," said Violet. She caught it and put it on the windowsill. "It's very pretty. I wonder where it came from—and the spider."

"Probably from Matilda. She's so messy!" said Ariana, feeling better now that the spider and the lizard were safely outside the dorm. "I bet she brought them in on her clothes. They're always covered in grass and stuff. Look—" She gestured toward the dirty clothes around Matilda's bed. "No wonder our dorm is full of bugs."

"Bugs? Who's got bugs?" Matilda yawned and opened her eyes. Reaching for her glasses, she accidentally knocked over her lucky duck toy. It immediately started quacking. "Whoops!" She picked it up and turned it this way and that. "I can never remember how to make this stop," she said, frowning.

Rosa buried her head under her pillow with a groan. "Turn it down!"

"Good thinking!" said Matilda cheerfully. She shoved the duck under her pillow, muffling the quacking noise. "So, what's going on?" she said, putting her glasses on and looking around at them all. "Why's the window open? It's freezing."

"A spider and a lizard decided to spend the night with us. We were just putting them outside," said Freya, shutting it.

"It's probably your fault." Ariana frowned at Matilda. "I bet they came in on your clothes and you didn't even notice. You're so messy! You really should fold your things and put them away." Matilda flopped back with a sigh, sending the toy duck shooting out from under her pillow. Its loud quacks sent Rosa, Freya, and Violet into a fit of giggles. Ariana felt hurt. She'd hoped the others would back her up. Surely they couldn't

enjoy sharing a dorm with someone as messy as Matilda?

As Ariana turned away, Violet put a hand on her arm. "Don't be upset, Ariana. I expect Matilda forgot to clean up last night because she was working on a picture."

"I was, actually," said Matilda, her long red hair falling over her shoulders as she nodded earnestly. "My little cousin was so excited when I told her all about being at school here. I promised I'd draw her a picture of our dorm. I've got it here somewhere, if you want to see." Matilda almost knocked a glass of water over as she began to sift through a pile of paper balanced on her dresser.

"You can show me later," said Ariana shortly. She sat down at the mirror. Her black hair was braided with colorful beads. She checked the beads were secure and tucked some braids behind her ear. Whatever Violet said, it wasn't

just last night that Matilda had forgotten to put her clothes away—she always forgot, and it was really annoying! Back at home, Ariana lived with just her mom and dad, and they were very clean and organized—just like Ariana. She had packed and repacked her suitcase several times before she left home to come to Unicorn Academy. She had been really looking forward to it, but she was finding it hard living in a dorm with four other girls, particularly messy Matilda.

Remembering the angry look Freya had given her when she'd carried the spider to the window, Ariana felt her stomach twist. Making friends was turning out to be so much harder than she had imagined. She hadn't thought the other girls would be so different from her! Violet was easy to get along with, but Freya spent much of her time alone with her engineering

inventions, Rosa always wanted to have adventures, and Matilda was annoyingly messy and scatterbrained. *I wish they were more like me,* thought Ariana wistfully. *I don't really feel like I've got any friends here at all.*

CHAPTER 2

After a delicious breakfast of pancakes and fresh fruit, Ariana was feeling better. She walked to the stables with the others, half-listening to their chatting, her hands buried in the pockets of her snuggly purple hoodie. She really did love Unicorn Academy. The spring sun was edging upward in the forget-me-not-blue sky, its rays making the marble towers and domed glass roof of the academy sparkle and shine. Ariana breathed a happy sigh as she thought about Whisper, the unicorn she had been paired with. He had big brown eyes and long eyelashes, his white coat was

patterned with trailing pink and blue flowers, and his dark pink mane was streaked with strands of a lighter pink and purple. Ariana thought he was the sweetest, most beautiful unicorn on Unicorn Island.

Like all the other girls and boys at Unicorn Academy, Ariana had joined the school in January, after she turned ten years old. Pupils usually stayed for a year, but if their unicorns hadn't yet discovered their unique magic and bonded with them, then they stayed for longer. Ariana couldn't wait for a lock of her hair to turn the same colors as Whisper's pink-and-purple mane. This would show that they'd bonded, which was the highest form of friendship.

Everyone at the academy was training to become guardians of Unicorn Island. Guardians protected everything on the island, especially the magical water that flowed from

11

Sparkle Lake around the land and kept all its animals healthy.

Usually, the island was very peaceful, but the year before, a group of students had defeated various wicked plans by Ms. Primrose, the school's head teacher, who had wanted to shut the academy down and take control of Sparkle Lake. Ms. Primrose had been caught and imprisoned, but the teachers knew she'd been working with an unknown person who'd still not been found. Ariana hoped there wasn't going to be any more trouble while she was at the academy.

Ahead of her, Rosa was chatting with Matilda and Violet. Freya was lost in her own thoughts.

"I can't wait until we go out on the cross-country course again," Rosa was saying. "I love cross-country jumping."

"Me too!" said Matilda. "Though I always get lost when Ms. Tulip makes us do a course. Do

you remember last time we went out? Pearl and I ended up stuck in the middle of a bog."

Violet grinned. "You looked like a mud monster afterward!"

Ariana shuddered at the memory. Matilda and Pearl had been covered from head to tail in thick, gloopy mud. It was the sort of thing she had nightmares about, but Matilda and the others had thought it was really funny.

Just then, two mice scurried out from behind a rosebush and dashed across the path, vanishing into the shadows beside some trees. Ariana jumped back in alarm—she'd never seen mice at the academy before. She was about to tell the others when she remembered Freya laughing at her for being scared of spiders. It was better not to say anything in case they teased her.

Ariana hurried into the stables. They were in a modern, airy building, beautifully clean and shiny,

and she loved it. Each unicorn had their own stall, and there were troughs that filled up with water from the lake to keep the unicorns' magic strong. Special carts moved around carrying hay and buckets of sky berries—the unicorns' favorite food.

As the girls entered the stables, Ariana wrinkled her nose. The air smelled strongly of stinky socks.

"Ariana! Watch out!" said Matilda suddenly. "There's a spider on you!"

"What? Where?" gasped Ariana, brushing her clothes frantically.

Matilda giggled. "Only joking!" Rosa chuckled too.

"Ignore them," Violet told Ariana. "You are so mean," she said, shaking her head at

14

Matilda, but there was a smile on her face.

Ariana stomped into Whisper's stall. She hated being teased. *It's not my fault I'm scared of spiders,* she thought angrily.

Whisper looked up from the hay net he was picking at and whinnied, his dark eyes lighting up. "Hello, Ariana," he said, coming over and nuzzling her face.

"Hello back," said Ariana, her anger fading away as she stroked his cheek. She hugged him and then sniffed. "Poo, what is that awful smell?"

"It's not me!" Whisper laughed. "I've stayed clean for once." Whisper loved going outside and having fun, and no matter how neat and tidy he started the day, he nearly always ended up covered in dirt.

Ariana fetched a brush. "I don't really mind if you get dirty. I like grooming you."

"So, what are we doing today?" Whisper asked her eagerly as she started to brush him. "I'm in the mood for galloping."

"It's Care of Unicorns first thing," said Ariana. "I think we're going to practice grooming and braiding."

Whisper groaned. "Not more grooming and braiding! Why can't we do something more fun? We're training to be guardians of the island, not to stand around looking pretty."

"Grooming and braiding *is* fun," said Ariana, brushing the tangles out of his mane. "It's important for guardians to look nice, and spending time together helps us bond."

"But we can also bond by galloping and having

adventures. If we have adventures, we might find out what my power is," said Whisper. He stamped a hoof impatiently. "I really want to discover my magic!"

"I know," said Ariana. "I want that too."

A little while ago, Rosa had discovered that her unicorn, Crystal, could make it snow and create wonderful snow twisters to whisk people from place to place. She'd bonded with Crystal soon after. Ariana thought being able to make it snow was a cool power. Maybe Whisper would have that too or, even better, a really useful power like being able to find things that were lost.

"I wonder what I'll be able to do. I'd like magic that means I can go really fast, or maybe fire magic or flying magic," said Whisper.

In the next stall, Matilda overheard. "I bet Ariana wants you to have cleaning magic, Whisper," she said.

Whisper made a face. "You don't wish I had something dull like that, do you, Ariana?"

Ariana blushed, glad he couldn't read her thoughts. "No, of course not," she said. "I don't care what you have. I'll love you anyway and always think you're the best unicorn in the world."

Whisper nuzzled her shoulder.

Ariana wrinkled her nose. "You know, that smell is getting even stronger."

Whisper sniffed the air. "You're right. It is."

"EEEEEEWWWWW!" There was a loud cry from the stall across the aisle from Whisper's.

"What's going on?" Ariana said in alarm.

She ran to the door, just in time to see Valentina, a second-year student, running out of Golden Briar's stall with a carrot in her hand. "In the straw!" she shrieked, pointing back at the stall dramatically. "Sleeping in Golden Briar's stall! EEEEEEEEK!"

"What is?" demanded Rosa. Everyone else came to their doors too.

"That!" shrieked Valentina as a large blue-and-gray storm raccoon, with blue fur ringing its eyes like a burglar's mask and a long stripy tail, appeared in Golden Briar's open doorway.

It spotted the carrot in Valentina's hand and sprang straight at her!

CHAPTER 3

Valentina shrieked as the storm raccoon bounded toward her. She threw the carrot at it, tripped over a bucket, and sat down in a pile of straw.

The raccoon caught the carrot, stuffed it in its mouth, and then scampered to the water trough. It leaped on top and swished its tail, dark eyes gleaming playfully.

"I'll catch it," called Miki from Topaz dorm, hurrying to the trough with his best friend, Himmat. "Stand back, everyone."

"Don't hurt it," called Violet anxiously.

"Don't worry. Miki's great with animals," said Himmat.

Miki produced a cookie from his pocket and held it out. The raccoon cocked its head, its blue-and-gray-ringed tail swishing as its eyes went from Miki to the cookie.

Speaking softly, Miki said, "Go on, take it. I'm not going to hurt you."

The raccoon hesitated then slowly reached out a paw.

"Don't feed it! We'll never get rid of it if you do!" Valentina exclaimed as she struggled up from the straw. She grabbed a striped rug hanging over a stable door and threw it over the raccoon. The startled creature let out a squeak as the rug fell over it, and it lost its balance, falling backward into the water trough, showering the nearby students with multicolored water.

The raccoon leaped out of the trough, splashing even more water, and charged around the stables. There was an uproar as some of the students chased after it, while others tried to keep out of the way. The unicorns whinnied, and Valentina screamed as the raccoon flew at her, using her head as a springboard to jump to

the ladder that led up to the hayloft.

"It touched my hair! Its smelly feet were on me!" screamed Valentina.

"Keep back," cried Violet anxiously. "You're scaring it!" She spread her arms wide to protect the raccoon, now scaling the ladder, with Miki climbing after it.

The raccoon didn't stop until it reached the trapdoor to the hayloft. Miki waited a few rungs below, holding up the cookie again. The raccoon peered down, chattering a warning each time Miki tried to climb higher. Miki froze, and for a long moment he and the raccoon stared at each other. Then the raccoon shook, and water from its fur sprayed Miki.

Miki burst out laughing, his dark brown eyes sparkling. The raccoon made a squeaky noise that sounded as if it was laughing too. It came down the ladder and jumped onto Miki's shoulder,

snatching the cookie from him. Miki stood very still, and the raccoon took a bite, its sharp teeth crunching noisily on the cookie.

"I'm telling a teacher," said Valentina, hands on her hips. "You shouldn't be feeding it, you stupid boy."

The raccoon chattered at Miki. "Mm, I agree," said Miki, pretending to understand. He grinned at Valentina. "It says you're the stupid one and that if I hadn't given it something to eat, we'd never have caught it. Oh, and it also says you've got straw on your butt."

There were shouts of laughter from everyone watching. Valentina's eyes narrowed, and she turned around and marched back into Golden Briar's stall in a huff.

"What is going on?" a voice cut through the laughter.

They all swung around to see Ms. Rosemary,

the Care of Unicorns teacher, and Ms. Rivers, the strict Geography and Culture teacher, standing in the stable entrance.

"Miki, why do you have a storm raccoon?" Ms. Rosemary said in surprise.

"We've just found it in the stables," said Miki.

Ms. Rivers frowned. "Well, you shouldn't be feeding it a cookie!"

"See?" said Valentina, poking her head out of the stall. "I tried telling him that, but he wouldn't listen. Raccoons are pests. They shouldn't be encouraged, should they?"

"It's not that," said Ms. Rivers, going over and stroking the raccoon. "Cookies are not good for storm raccoons' digestion. It'd be better to feed it something less sweet."

"Well done for catching it, dear," Ms. Rosemary said to Miki. "Now, why don't you take it back to the woods and release it there? I wonder what it's

doing here in school. They hardly ever venture out of the trees."

Miki set off with the raccoon.

"Everyone else, back to grooming your unicorns, please," said Ms. Rosemary.

Ariana ducked inside Whisper's stall, feeling glad that she hadn't gotten as wet as some of the others. She picked up the brush again.

"Something's not right," she overheard Ms. Rivers say to Ms. Rosemary. "There have been several sightings of wild animals, birds, and insects around the academy today. Now there's a storm raccoon too."

Ariana remembered the spider and the lizard in Diamond dorm and the mice she'd seen on her way to the stables. She hurried and told the teachers. Both Ms. Rivers and Ms. Rosemary listened carefully.

"Thank you, Ariana, that's very useful to know," said Ms. Rosemary.

"I will add these creatures to the list of sightings," said Ms. Rivers. "They must have come out of the woods."

"Why?" asked Ariana.

"That is not your concern," said Ms. Rivers firmly. "We teachers will deal with it." She marched away.

Ms. Rosemary gave Ariana a friendly smile. "Don't worry about it, dear. We'll soon find out what's going on." She clapped her hands together. "Okay, everyone, we've had a lot of excitement already this morning, so I think we'll go on a relaxing ride around the grounds. Put your grooming things away and assemble in the yard with your unicorns."

Rosa, Violet, and Matilda high-fived each

other, but Ariana's heart sank. She would really rather spend the time making the braids in Whisper's mane perfect than riding around the grounds getting muddy.

Whisper whickered happily. "Hooray! We get to go out!" he said, stamping his hooves.

"Yes," Ariana sighed. "We do."

As Ms. Rosemary led her class on a ride around Sparkle Lake, even Ariana couldn't keep

wishing they'd stayed in the stables. The spring flowers were blooming in the flower beds—a combination of pink, lilac, and purple—and the sunshine was making the lake glitter brightly. The marble academy building was reflected in the glassy surface. It was so clear that it looked as if there was a second Unicorn Academy floating right there in the water.

Ariana listened to the cheerful chatting of her roommates as she rode with them, but most

of her attention was taken up in making sure that Whisper didn't tread in the mud around the lake.

Ms. Rosemary directed everyone along a path through the rose gardens that led to the maze and the playground at the edge of the woods. There she stopped and checked her watch.

"You have fifteen minutes of free time to do what you want while I check the woods for any unusual animal behavior," she said.

The rest of Diamond dorm and their unicorns headed for the playground.

"Let's go with them, Ariana," said Whisper eagerly.

Ariana hesitated. So far, she'd managed to avoid going to the playground. Every time her roommates played on the equipment, they came back covered in dirt.

"I'd really like to go to the maze again," said Ariana. "I like it in there."

"But the maze is boring if you go in it alone," protested Whisper. "I want to go to the playground with the others. Please, Ariana, pleeeeease!"

Ariana didn't want to disappoint Whisper. "Okay then," she agreed reluctantly.

"Hooray!" Whisper whinnied, setting off at a canter. "Let's go on the trampoline first."

"I don't really want to," said Ariana, looking at the mud around it. She slid off his back. "You go, though."

"Well, if you're sure?" said Whisper. When she nodded, he cantered over to join his friends on the trampolines, leaving Ariana alone.

Ariana glanced around. Matilda was sitting at the top of the fort, her pencil skittering over her sketch pad as she captured something on

paper. Violet and Rosa were on the swings, seeing how high they could go. Freya was climbing the rock wall, while the unicorns played on the trampolines. Ariana didn't feel like joining in with any of them, so she went and sat on the wooden flying unicorn statue.

As she sat there, she began to think about all the insects and animals from the woods that had been found at the academy. A horrible thought struck her: What if some of the really dangerous creatures turned up at the academy—a wolf, a giant scarlet-horned cobra, or a swarm of hex hornets?

Ariana was still deep in thought when something moved under the merry-go-round, catching her eye. Her heart beat double-time. Was it another animal? A breeze blew, and the creature came tumbling out of its hiding place toward Ariana. She gasped, but then stopped herself from squealing just in time.

It wasn't an animal at all, just a large leaf! Ariana giggled, feeling a little silly. But as she started to relax, something whizzed past her ear. Was that a hornet? As Ariana batted it away, she lost her balance and toppled from the unicorn's back, her arms flailing as she fell. Somehow, she landed on her feet. From the top of the fort, Matilda cheered and waved her sketch pad. Violet and Rosa, who'd also seen what happened, ran over.

"Are you all right?" asked Violet, steadying the trembling Ariana. "What happened? Did the

butterfly surprise you?" She pointed to a large purple butterfly swooping around the playground.

"A butterfly?" *Is that all it was?*

"Are you scared of butterflies as well as spiders?" Rosa asked.

"No, of course not," said Ariana. "I . . . I thought it was a hornet." She blushed and rubbed at the smudge she'd just noticed on the sleeve of her hoodie. From the top of the fort, she could hear Matilda chuckling.

Ariana felt like stamping her foot. "I'm not scared of butterflies!" she shouted. She turned and stomped away from them.

Next time, I get to decide what Whisper and I do, she thought angrily. *And it won't be going to the playground with the others!*

CHAPTER 4

To Ariana's relief, the rest of the day was less eventful. By bedtime, there'd only been one other sighting of an animal from the woods that had wandered onto the school grounds, a timid three-antlered deer.

From her bedroom window, Ariana saw one of the gardeners lead the deer away. Ariana closed the curtains and went to the bathroom. When she came back, everyone was crowded around Matilda's bed, their heads close together as they giggled over something. Seeing Ariana, Violet nudged the others, and they all pulled away, returning to their

own beds. Ariana wondered what they'd been looking at.

"Hi, Ariana," said Violet quickly. "We wondered where you'd gone. Would you like a piece of chocolate? It's got a strawberry filling." She held out an opened bar of chocolate.

"No, thanks. I've just brushed my teeth."

"I'd better brush mine," said Matilda. Her cheeks were pink, and she was holding something behind her back, before quickly shoving it into a drawer. "Now, where did I put my washbag?"

"Is this it?" Ariana picked up a flowery bag stuffed halfway inside a fluffy cat slipper that she'd just noticed was under her bed.

"Yes, it is!" Matilda replied, not quite meeting Ariana's eye. "And that's my cat slipper! I've been hopping around all week without it. Thanks, Ariana."

Matilda set off to the bathroom, and the rest of

Diamond dorm followed her, clutching washbags and toothbrushes. Left on her own, Ariana stared at the pile of Matilda's clothes heaped on the floor. It was as much of a mess as it had been that morning. Carefully, shaking them out to check for spiders first, she picked the clothes up and put them on Matilda's bed.

Matilda was *so* messy. She hadn't even bothered to shut her drawer properly. But as Ariana leaned over to close it, she noticed something sticking out from the top, a drawing of a girl with braids. Ariana froze. Was that her? She pulled it out. It was her—there was no doubt about it. Matilda was a very good artist. Too good! Ariana's eyes watered as she studied the way Matilda had captured her, arms waving wildly, her mouth a huge O of surprise. In the picture, Ariana looked truly terrified as she sat atop a winged unicorn while a butterfly flew around her head.

Is that how the rest of Diamond dorm saw her—a scaredy-cat, frightened even of butterflies? Ariana shoved the picture into the drawer and slammed it shut. She got into bed, pulled the blanket up to her chin, and shut her eyes tight. When the rest of Diamond dorm came back from the bathroom, Ariana pretended to be fast asleep.

The following morning, Ariana came in from the bathroom to find Rosa sitting on Matilda's bed, giggling over a picture in her sketch pad. Ariana stiffened. Was it another drawing of her? She was beginning to really wish she was in another dorm.

"Look at this!" Rosa said, holding the picture up. It was a picture of Matilda after she'd been stuck in the bog on the cross-country ride. Her hair was hanging in mucky straggles, and she had mud dripping off her nose. "And there's

one of Freya." She held up a picture of Freya looking like a mad inventor, blond hair sticking out wildly as she tinkered with a machine. "And she did one of me too!" She held up another picture. It showed Rosa with her hands on her hips, nose in the air, bossing everyone

around. It was a very good likeness. "You are so good at drawing," Rosa told Matilda. She posed like her picture. "It's just like me when I'm in a bossy mood. Isn't it, Ariana?"

Ariana didn't say anything, feeling it would be rude to agree. She sat down on her bed, her thoughts racing. Last night she'd thought Matilda had been mean to draw that picture of her, but she'd actually been doing pictures of everyone in the dorm and no one else seemed to mind. In fact, judging by their grins, they all thought it was funny.

"I've got one of you too, Ariana," said Matilda shyly. "Do you want to see it?"

Ariana nodded, and Matilda pulled the drawing from her dresser. Ariana tensed, waiting to feel hurt like she had the night before, but to her surprise she didn't feel upset. Now that she knew Matilda was drawing everyone, she was

actually able to see how funny the picture was.

"It's good," she admitted. "Really good." Matilda looked pleased. "But I'm not actually scared of butterflies, you know," Ariana added.

"Duh! I know that!" said Matilda, rolling her eyes.

Ariana folded her pajamas, feeling slightly confused. She really didn't understand Matilda, but she was starting to see that her teasing wasn't meant to hurt. Maybe she shouldn't take it so seriously. She shot Matilda a tentative smile. "Do you want help folding your clothes, or are you going for the crumpled look on purpose?"

Matilda looked surprised for a moment, but then chuckled. "I think Ms. Rosemary would prefer the less crumpled look, so yes, please!"

Together, they picked up her clothes and folded them. By the time Ariana went down

to breakfast with the others, she was feeling a lot lighter inside.

Breakfast was almost finished when, at the teachers' table, Ms. Nettles, the head teacher, stood up and clapped her hands together. Silence rippled around the room as the students turned to face her.

"I'm sorry to announce that today's lessons are canceled." Ms. Nettles's lips twitched as everyone started to whisper excitedly. "The teachers and I have decided that the whole school is going on a field trip."

Rosa put up her hand. "Where to, Ms. Nettles?"

"To the woods!" Ms. Nettles declared. A ripple of excitement ran around the room. Ms. Nettles raised her hand, and silence fell again. "Over the last couple of days, there have been

many sightings in and around the school of creatures that don't belong here," she said. "In fact, only this morning a family of purple badgers were discovered near the map in the Great Hall. We need to find out why the animals are coming out of the woods. The plan is for all students to ride to the outskirts of the woods to help conduct a survey of the animals, so that we can begin to chart which animals are leaving and why."

"Only to the outskirts, Ms. Nettles?" Matilda asked.

"Absolutely!" Ms. Nettles fixed all the students with a stern look from over the top of her glasses. "Please remember there are some extremely dangerous

creatures in the woods. Staff may venture farther into the trees, but students must stay near the edge. Ms. Rivers will lead the expedition. After breakfast, please assemble by the lake, where you will be given the equipment you need."

Ariana felt a shiver of fear. Usually the woods were out of bounds to students.

Beside her, Matilda was looking excited. "No lessons and a trip to the woods—how utterly exciting!" she said, pushing her red hair out of her glasses.

Rosa was beaming from ear to ear. "Another adventure—I can't wait!"

CHAPTER 5

Diamond dorm chatted excitedly together as they finished breakfast. Even Freya, who was usually too busy with her inventions to join in, took part in the discussion. Only Ariana was quiet. She really wasn't excited about the expedition. Of course, if there was some reason the animals were leaving the woods, then they needed to find out why. But surely a whole school trip needed more planning? Would the teachers be able to supervise them properly and keep them all safe? Finishing her breakfast, she told the others she would see them in the dorm and hurried

upstairs. If they were going out, she wanted to be prepared!

"Ariana, you look like you're going away for a week!" said Violet, when Ariana met them all at the stables later. Although she had been first to the dorm to get ready, she had been so busy packing stuff into a backpack to take with her that she had been the last to get to the stables.

"Have you got a spare unicorn hidden in there?" Matilda giggled.

"It's important to be ready for anything," Ariana said defensively.

"What have you got?" said Violet.

"Rope, a flashlight, some sky berries, chocolate, a fishing net . . ."

"A fishing net!" Matilda echoed.

Rosa chuckled. "You really are Little Miss Organized, aren't you?"

Ariana hesitated, but, to her surprise, Freya came to her defense. "Ariana's right—it is better to be prepared. We don't know what we'll find in the woods."

"Excitement and danger, I hope!" said Rosa, her brown eyes shining.

Ariana frowned as she went to Whisper's stall.

When everyone was ready, Ms. Rosemary and Ms. Rivers put the students into groups. Ms. Willow, the school nurse, was there too, giving out sandwiches for lunch, a whistle to call for help if they needed it, and a small first aid kit. "Be

careful," she was telling the students. "I really don't think this trip is wise." She shot an angry look at Ms. Rosemary and Ms. Rivers. "It could be very dangerous in the woods. Make sure you stay on the outskirts."

"We'll be fine, Ms. Willow," Violet said. "Don't worry."

Ms. Willow huffed and hurried away.

Ms. Rosemary handed out a list of creatures that they were supposed to check off if they saw them. Diamond dorm was the last group she came to.

"Now, remember what Ms. Nettles said at breakfast," she told them as she handed them their list. "Please do not go deep into the woods. I know you had a great adventure when you went to the Glittering Cavern a few weeks ago, but if you go off exploring on your own again, you could get hurt. The woods are dangerous. Stay near the edge, do you understand?"

"Yes, Ms. Rosemary," said Rosa with a sigh. "We understand."

Ariana remembered how excited Rosa had been leading their secret expedition to the Glittering Cavern last month. They'd been trying to find a model taken from the school's magic map that was needed for the map to work again. They'd found it and gotten back safely—but only just!

"Time to go!" called Ms. Rivers. She led the way on Lady, her unicorn, who had a stunning gold mane and gold-and-pink markings. The rest of the school followed, with teachers dotted at various intervals and Diamond dorm and Ms. Rosemary bringing up the rear.

"Please avoid the mud, Whisper," Ariana begged as they followed Matilda and Rosa toward the woods.

The other unicorns were splashing through the puddles on the ground. "We are probably going to get quite muddy, Ariana," said Whisper as he skirted around them.

"Oh, I hope not!" said Ariana with a shudder.

"Hey! Come and ride with us, Ariana," Matilda called over her shoulder.

"We're talking about that story we read in Unicorn Myths and Legends class," said Rosa. Pearl shifted to let Whisper trot up between her and Crystal.

"About the unicorn and the Cyclops? I loved that story," said Ariana, forgetting about the mud as she eagerly joined in. "My favorite part was when the unicorn with the gold hooves—" Ariana broke off suddenly. Coming toward them was a long line of rabbits, their tails flashing white as they hopped along. "Where are they going?" she wondered aloud.

Rosa frowned. "They look like they're running away from the woods."

"I wonder why." Bubbles of anxiety popped in Ariana's stomach. What was making the rabbits leave the safety of the trees?

Ms. Rivers halted Lady. "Well, here are the woods, everyone. Start looking for animals. If you need help, blow three sharp blasts on your whistle and we will come find you. Be sensible. We simply need you to note what animals you see. Do you understand?" Everyone nodded. "Then off you go!"

With a chorus of whoops, the groups set off.

"Race you to the trees, Diamond dorm! Watch out for the rabbits," Rosa shouted as she and Crystal took off at top speed. Freya and Honey chased after them, followed by the rest of Diamond dorm.

Not wanting to be left behind, Whisper broke

into a gallop, his mane flying up in Ariana's face.

"Whoa, slow down. I'm going to fall off!" Ariana cried out.

"Relax, Ariana. You know you can't fall off. The island magic will keep you safe!" said Whisper, and he galloped faster. Ariana knew he was right. If she fell, a magical bubble would

form around her, cushioning and protecting her, but that didn't help her feel safe as they entered the woods. Falling off wasn't her main concern—it was all the dangers they might face if they went too far in.

"This is so much fun!" said Rosa gleefully, slowing to a walk.

"I love adventures!" said Matilda, taking her sketch pad out and starting to sketch.

"I vote we go down that path and then start looking for animals," Freya said, pointing to the left.

Ariana pulled the whistle out of her backpack, just in case she might need it. She glanced around, her eyes scanning for danger.

Suddenly, Rosa and Crystal stopped. Ariana fell forward, banging her nose on Whisper's neck. "What are you doing?" she exclaimed.

"Quiet!" hissed Rosa.

Ariana looked in front of Rosa and froze. On the path in front of them, there was an enormous scarlet-horned cobra snake. It reared up, its blue hood spread out wide and its mouth open, showing a flickering tongue and pointed yellow fangs!

CHAPTER 6

"A scarlet-horned cobra," Ariana breathed. She'd never seen one in real life before, but she knew they were very dangerous.

The snake was right in the middle of the path. Its tiny black eyes glinted with menace as it uttered a long warning hiss.

"What do we do?" whispered Rosa.

"We could turn around," said Ariana. "After all, we're not supposed to be going far into the woods."

"We can't turn around yet!" said

Matilda. "We've hardly come in any way at all."

"We could try and trap it so we can get past," said Freya. "All we need is a branch with a forked end and a piece of string. Luckily I brought some string with me." She slipped her backpack off and rummaged inside, pulling out a length of string.

Ariana couldn't believe her ears! How could Freya even think about catching the cobra?

"We haven't got time for you to make something, Freya," said Violet anxiously as the snake started to sway menacingly from side to side. The unicorns skittered backward. "Steady, Twinkle," she soothed her unicorn.

"We need to make it go away," said Rosa.

Before Ariana could stop him, Whisper trotted forward and stamped his hoof at the snake. "Shoo!"

A spark seemed to fly up from his hoof, and Ariana's nose caught the faint smell of burnt

sugar. The scarlet-horned cobra shut its mouth and sank down toward the ground. For a moment, she thought it was going to do what Whisper had said, but then it suddenly reared up again and struck out. Whisper leaped back in alarm as the snake's fangs missed his nose by inches.

"It really doesn't seem to want to go!" he said, retreating to a safe distance. The snake swayed angrily on the spot. Ariana gulped.

"If only we could frighten it away," said Rosa.

"But how do you frighten a snake?" said Matilda.

"They don't like bright lights," said Freya.

"Light!" gasped Ariana. She pulled her backpack off and rummaged for the flashlight she had packed. "Let's see what happens when I do this. . . ." Taking a breath, she switched on her flashlight and shined it straight into the snake's mean eyes. It recoiled with a hiss and shrank back.

"It's working!" cried Violet.

With a final hiss, the snake sank to the floor and slithered quickly away.

Matilda whooped. "Way to go, Ariana! That was a seriously scary snake. You were really brave."

Ariana glowed.

Matilda shot a grin at her. "Lucky it wasn't a butterfly!"

Ariana smiled back, for once not bothered by the teasing.

"That was awesome, Ariana," said Rosa warmly. "Come on, everyone!" She urged Crystal on, and they cantered away down the path. The others charged after her. Ariana's heart was

beating fast, but although she still felt nervous, she also felt fired up and excited. She'd gotten rid of a snake! The others thought she was brave!

"Isn't this fun?" said Whisper happily to her as his hooves pounded on the track.

Ariana hesitated. "It is," she said cautiously. "But I don't think we should go too much farther in." She raised her voice. "Rosa! Remember we're supposed to stay near the edge of the woods."

Rosa slowed down to a walk. "I guess," she said reluctantly.

"We could stop here," said Violet, looking around. They were on a wide path with a thick canopy of branches overhead. "We could get out the list and start ticking off the animals we see."

"And eat our sandwiches." Matilda grinned. They all dismounted from their unicorns and took their sandwiches out of their backpacks.

"Yum!" said Rosa, biting into a ham sandwich. "I wish lessons were canceled every day."

Ariana nibbled on the crust of her sandwich. She wasn't that hungry. She didn't like being in the woods, and she wanted to get out as soon as possible. She took the list out of her bag and started checking off every creature she saw— a squirrel climbing a branch, a hedgehog in the leaves, a robin in the trees. . . .

When the girls had finished eating, they lay

on their backs in the grass while Ariana perched awkwardly on a rock and kept a lookout.

"Check crows off the list," Rosa said to Ariana as three huge crows with sharp beaks swooped from the trees to peck at the sandwich crumbs.

As Ariana put the remains of her sandwich into her backpack, the largest bird hopped toward her.

"Shoo!" She flapped her arms at it.

The crow fixed her with a stare and hopped closer.

"Go on, shoo!" Ariana clapped her hands.

The bird fluffed out its feathers and looked at her with its beady eyes. It didn't seem scared at all. Whisper broke away from the other unicorns and came to stand beside her. He locked eyes with the bird and stamped his hoof on the ground.

"Go away!" he told it.

Ariana caught a whiff of a sweet smell like

burnt sugar. The crow's feathers flattened, and it backed away. Whisper stamped his hoof again, and a spark flew up.

Ariana frowned. "Whisper, did you just make that spark? Could it be your magic?"

She squealed and ducked as the crow suddenly flew up and flapped at her face. It snatched the sandwich from her hand with its scaly talons before cawing triumphantly and swooping into the trees.

Whisper snorted in alarm. "Horrible bird."

"It's taken the rest of my sandwich!" said Ariana in dismay.

"That's really weird," said Freya. "Birds are usually scared of humans."

Ariana looked around uneasily. There were rustlings in the bushes. Maybe something else was planning to attack them?

"Look! Look over there!" said Rosa. She pointed

into the trees. "There's something moving! An animal—a large one."

"What type of animal?" said Violet.

"I don't know." Rosa's eyes gleamed. "But I think we should follow it and find out!"

"No," said Ariana. "We're supposed to stay on the outskirts of the woods."

"We're not that far in," said Rosa. She hurried over to Crystal. "And we are supposed to be noting every animal we see. Who votes we go after it?"

The others all raised their hands, and the unicorns nodded eagerly.

"It's decided then," said Rosa bossily.

Ariana swallowed as they all jumped onto their unicorns. She wished the others hadn't voted for Rosa's plan. She really didn't want to go farther into the forest!

As Diamond dorm went deeper into the trees trying to catch up with the animal Rosa had

seen, the woods became noisy with chatters and squeaks. There were lots of mysterious rustles coming from the bushes, and Ariana felt shivers starting to run down her spine.

"Whisper," said Ariana softly. "I feel like something is wrong in the woods."

"What do you mean?" Whisper looked around. "I can't see anything strange."

Ariana saw two squirrels watching them from a nearby tree. Squirrels were usually cute, but these two were staring in a strange way. "Look at those squirrels."

But as Whisper followed her gaze, the squirrels scampered away. "They look normal to me," he said. "Stop worrying. We're having an adventure—enjoy it!"

Ariana bit her lip. Maybe she was just being overly careful. Whisper trotted after the others, but just as he joined them, they all heard a loud

howling and snarling noise. "What's that?" said Pearl, stopping.

"A wolf and a bear!" gasped Violet as the two animals came charging out of the trees.

A huge wolf and a gray bear faced each other. The bear had two small cubs with it. The adult animals circled around each other, teeth bared.

"They're going to fight!" said Freya.

"We need to stop them," said Violet, her voice wobbling. "We can't let them hurt each other— we're guardians of the island."

"It's too dangerous," Ariana protested.

The wolf and the bear lunged at each other, snarling and growling.

"Stop it!" Whisper stamped a hoof on the floor. Blue and yellow sparks flew upward, and the same smell of burnt sugar filled the air.

"Whisper!" gasped Ariana. "It *is* you making those sparks!"

The wolf, who had been crouched and ready to spring, all of a sudden seemed to lose concentration. Its nose twitched, and it sniffed the air. The bear dropped down onto all fours. Shaking its head, it stared at the unicorn. Whisper looked at his hoof as if he couldn't quite believe what had happened. He stamped it again, and even more sparks shot up. The bear and the wolf both relaxed, the tension leaving them.

"Please leave each other alone," said Whisper. "Be friends. Don't fight."

The wolf trotted up to the bear, licked its nose and bounded away. The bear shuffled over to its cubs, nuzzled them, and with a last look at Whisper, ambled away happily into the trees with the cubs scampering beside it.

Ariana realized she and the others were all staring after them with sweet expressions on their faces.

"Ah, how sweet," breathed Freya.

"So cute," Violet added.

Ariana blinked. The smell of burnt sugar was strong. She was sure she knew what was going on. "Whisper! You've found your powers! You've got soothing magic."

Whisper looked shocked and delighted. "Soothing magic is used to calm animals and people, and make them be friends. It's not a showy magic, but it's very useful."

"I think it's wonderful," said Ariana. "You just saved those animals from getting hurt." Relief rushed through her. She could definitely cope with a unicorn with soothing magic—it was so much better than something scary and unpredictable like fire magic.

She hugged Whisper. "I'm so proud of you!"

Whisper nuzzled her shoulder. "Have we bonded?"

"I don't know." Ariana tilted her head, the beads in her braids clacking as she looked for a purple-and-pink streak in her black hair. "Not yet," she added, hiding her disappointment. "But you got your magic. That's so cool!"

"It's awesome!" Matilda cried, coming over to them, blinking out of the peaceful, trancelike state Whisper's magic had put her into.

"I'm so happy for you both," said Violet. "And we're much safer with Whisper's magic. He'll be able to stop any dangerous animals from hurting us."

Ariana nodded, but she remembered what Ms. Rosemary had said in their first ever Care of Unicorns lesson. The teacher had warned the class that performing magic was very tiring and not to expect too much of their unicorns, especially when their magic first appeared. Would Whisper have the energy to calm another fierce animal if they met one?

"Let's keep going," said Rosa. "And keep your eyes peeled for more animals."

They continued along the path. They hadn't gone much farther when Ariana had the same feeling that something was wrong. She stiffened and swung around, then smiled in relief. It was just a group of chipmunks. They had come out from the bushes and were trotting after them. A fox and two raccoons joined them. They were all staring at the girls.

"Um, everyone, have you seen what's

happening behind us?" said Ariana, anxious now. The animals looked a bit strange. It was the way their gazes never wavered, like the squirrels she had seen earlier. The others all looked and stopped.

"It's like we're playing follow-the-leader," Matilda observed as a pink porcupine with sharp quills came out too, followed by four wolves, a group of mice, and a three-antlered deer.

"How weird! Why are they all following us?" said Rosa.

"Maybe they're hungry?" Violet suggested. "And they think we have some food?"

Freya cut her off. "Um, I don't want to worry anyone, but we've been surrounded."

Ariana realized she was right. While they had been standing still, even more animals had come out from the trees and encircled them. Ariana looked around nervously. The animals were all

staring fixedly at the girls and their unicorns, not making a sound.

"What are they doing?" said Violet nervously. "Why are they watching us like that?"

The animals began to advance on the girls and their unicorns.

"They're under a spell!" cried Freya. "Someone must have used dark magic on them!"

"Let's get out of here, everyone!" shouted Rosa. She urged Crystal on. Crystal galloped straight at a gap between the deer and a wolf. The watching animals lunged at her, but Crystal galloped past them, leaping in the air to avoid their teeth and claws.

"Come on!" Rosa shrieked to the others. "Quick!"

CHAPTER 7

The other unicorns charged after Crystal and thundered down the forest path. The enchanted animals chased them. Branches snagged on Ariana's clothes, and dirt flew up in her face.

"Faster," she urged, not caring when her hoodie ripped. Glancing behind, she could see the animals still pursuing them. The wolves' howls echoed toward her.

"Hold tight," Whisper panted as he galloped toward a fallen tree that was lying across the path.

Ariana leaned forward, sliding her hands up Whisper's neck as he flew over it. He landed, but

then suddenly slammed on the brakes. They skidded along in the mud, stopping when they crashed into Matilda and Pearl. Ariana was catapulted over Whisper's head. For a second, she was flying toward a tree, but suddenly a huge bubble shimmered in the air around her. She bobbed inside it, a few inches above the ground, and then she found herself floating back to Whisper. Once she was safely sitting on his back, the bubble popped.

"Eek!" Ariana almost wished she could have stayed in the bubble—she'd felt much safer inside it.

Ahead of them

was a muddy river. Crystal had stopped too late and skidded into it. She was thrashing around in the water, trying to find her feet and get out while Rosa clung to her back. Freya's and Violet's unicorns were at the edge of the river, up to their knees in mud, shouting encouragement.

"We're trapped!" exclaimed Matilda to Ariana in alarm.

Looking behind them, Ariana saw the animals racing along the path toward them, getting closer and closer, their teeth showing, their claws unsheathed.

Crystal staggered out of the water, her sides heaving as she gasped for breath. She was safe, but Ariana knew there was no time for her to gather her magic power to transport them away in a snow twister.

"Whisper," said Ariana urgently. "Can you use your soothing magic?"

"I might be able to calm some of them, but I don't think I'm strong enough to take them all on," said Whisper, trembling as he looked at the amber-eyed wolves leading the pack.

Ariana leaned forward and hugged Whisper tightly. He was their only hope. The howling was filling her ears now, and her skin prickled with fear. "Please try. I know you can do it, Whisper."

"I'll do my best," said Whisper. "Please stay by me—I feel braver when you're with me."

Ariana stroked Whisper's neck. "I'm not going anywhere. We're in this together."

She felt his muscles tense as he lowered his head, pawing the riverbank with one hoof before striking the ground with it. "Stop! We're your friends!" he called as the animals surged over the fallen log. A flurry of colored sparkles exploded up from the ground and showered down on the heads of the snarling creatures. Eyes flashed and

glowed, then gradually the glow faded and they turned dreamy, their roars and growls softening at the same time. They slowed to a stop.

"I'm so tired!" Whisper gasped.

"But you've done it," Ariana told him in delight. "Look, the animals are turning back to normal!"

The animals were shaking their heads in confusion, looking as if they didn't know what they were doing there. They started to amble away, disappearing into the bushes and trees. A young red fox lagged behind. Once or twice it stopped to look back, but finally it disappeared into the undergrowth.

"You did it, Whisper!" Violet said in delight. "You made them friendly again."

Ariana slid from Whisper's back as he staggered.

"What's the matter?" Ariana asked him in alarm.

He sunk to his knees in the mud, breathing heavily. "Doing that magic has used up all my energy."

Ariana flung herself down beside him and hugged him. If only she had something that would help him! She suddenly realized she did. She'd packed a bag of sky berries along with the other just-in-case things in her backpack. Sky berries were good at giving unicorns their energy back after doing magic. She pulled the bag out of her backpack.

"Here," said Ariana, offering the sky berries to Whisper. "Eat these."

Ariana fed the sky berries to Whisper one at a time until his breathing slowed and the sparkle returned to his dark eyes. "Thank you," he said gratefully, standing up and shaking himself. His white coat was streaked with mud. "I almost

feel normal again. I'm so glad you thought of bringing those sky berries. You're the best."

Ariana hugged him tightly, her heart swelling with love. She was filthy from crouching in the mud, but she didn't care. The only thing that mattered was Whisper.

He nuzzled her. "I'm sorry I didn't believe you, earlier—about things seeming strange in here. I was sure you were imagining things."

"It's okay," said Ariana. "I know I'm always super careful and overcautious."

"Well, I'm very glad you're so organized," said Whisper. "And I'm sorry you got all muddy."

"I don't care," she said. "I'm just glad you're feeling better now."

"We have to find out why the animals are all behaving so strangely," said Rosa.

"It's really odd," said Freya. "The animals who live in these woods are supposed to be very shy.

Even the fierce ones usually avoid people."

"Look!" Matilda pointed. "The fox cub is back."

The little fox was staring intently at Matilda from around the side of a tree. Then it ducked back. Seconds later it reappeared. When the fox vanished then reappeared for the third time, Matilda suddenly understood.

"I think it wants us to follow it."

Excitement flashed in Rosa's eyes. "Maybe it needs help. It might be trying to show us why the animals are behaving so strangely."

"Shouldn't we tell a teacher rather than follow it?" said Ariana.

"There's no time to call for a teacher. The fox might not wait. I think we should follow it. Who's with me?" asked Rosa.

"Me!" chorused everyone except Ariana.

"I really think we should," said Whisper quietly.

81

Ariana wasn't very happy, but she trusted Whisper and didn't want to let him down. She and Whisper set off with the others after the fox cub. It went at a fast pace, but every now and then it slowed to check that the girls were still following.

After a while, Crystal lifted her head. "I think I can smell water in that direction," she said, looking farther down the path.

"Me too," said Pearl.

"I wonder," said Rosa thoughtfully. "There's a magical waterfall in the middle of these woods—the Verdant Falls. There's a pool at the bottom and a stream where the animals drink. Do you think the fox cub is taking us there?"

"It looks like it," said Freya. "Maybe there's a problem with the water, and that's why the animals are behaving weirdly?"

Ariana bit her lip as Rosa, Matilda, and Violet nodded. If the fox was taking them to the waterfall,

then it would mean going even deeper into the woods, exactly what they'd been told not to do. However, if there was something wrong with the water, then they really needed to know, especially as future guardians of Unicorn Island.

"Ariana? Are you still okay?" Whisper asked.

"Yes," she answered firmly.

Whisper nuzzled her leg. "Good, because I'll look after you," he promised.

"We'll look after each other," she said, hugging him tightly.

CHAPTER 8

The unicorns headed through the trees. As they trotted down the path, Ariana heard the sound of trickling water.

"Do you think that's the Verdant Falls?" Matilda said.

Freya frowned. "No. The Verdant Falls is a really powerful waterfall. I've seen pictures in books. The water comes flowing out of a hole in a cliff face and lands in a pool. It would make a much louder noise than that."

"I can definitely smell water this way," said Crystal, sniffing the air again.

They rounded a bend and stopped. Ahead of them was a rocky cliff face. A tiny stream of water was trickling out of a cave near the top. It was falling into a sludgy brown pool at the bottom. The fox walked to the edge of the pool. Then it looked at the girls.

"Is that the magic waterfall?" asked Rosa in surprise. "It's not very impressive."

"It can't be the Verdant Falls," said Freya. "There isn't enough water." She looked around. "Everything else looks the same as the pictures though—the cliff, the pool at the bottom . . ." She trailed off. "I'm sure this is the falls, but what's happened to it?"

Ariana caught her breath. "Maybe someone has done something to stop the water flowing properly."

The fox pricked its large red ears.

"You're very friendly, aren't you?" said

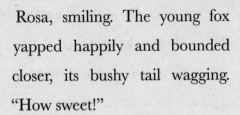

Rosa, smiling. The young fox yapped happily and bounded closer, its bushy tail wagging. "How sweet!"

The fox cub rolled over onto its back to have its fluffy tummy tickled, and Rosa got off Crystal to stroke it. After a while, the cub got to its feet and ran to the pool. The girls and their unicorns watched as it lapped up a few mouthfuls of water with its pink tongue. As the cub swallowed, it stiffened. It looked around at them, and the hackles on the back of its neck rose. Lowering its head, the cub bared its teeth and snarled. Its eyes glowed, and then it pounced.

Whisper instantly stamped his hoof. Sparks flew up and landed on the cub's head. With a

surprised bark, it skidded to a halt. The glow faded from its eyes. The cub shook its head. Whining in confusion, it trotted over to the girls.

Rosa crouched down and patted it. "You clever thing," she said. "You're trying to tell us that there's something wrong with the water."

Ariana stroked Whisper. "Well done. Are you okay?"

He nodded. "The cub was smart enough not to drink too much water, so I only had to use a little bit of magic. We've got to do something though, Ariana. We can't let the animals all turn bad!"

"I know," she said.

Violet and Matilda had dismounted and were making a fuss over the little fox cub with Rosa. Meanwhile, Freya had gotten off Honey and was examining the water. "Someone might have put a dark magic spell on this pool, and there's no fresh water to wash it clean," she said, wading through

the shallow water at the edge. She turned over the nearby rocks and boulders. "There may be some clues somewhere. Come and help me look." The others joined her, but Ariana hesitated. It looked very muddy and wet.

"Why don't we go to the top of the cliff, Ariana, and see if we can find anything up there?" said Whisper. "We might find out why the water isn't flowing properly out of the cave."

"Okay." Ariana liked that idea far better than rooting around in the mud. She told the others what they were doing. "We'll go up there," she said, pointing to a path that led up to the top of the cliff.

"All right, shout if you find anything," said Rosa.

Whisper followed the path up the cliff. When they were nearly at the top, Ariana dismounted and they cautiously approached the cliff edge

so they could look down at the hole the water should be flowing from. Whisper's hooves slipped on the wet rocks as he got closer to the edge.

"Wait!" Ariana said. "It's not safe. Have you seen how steep the drop is to the pool below? You stay here, and I'll go on. I can crawl."

"Are you sure?" said Whisper. "You'll get wet and dirty."

"I don't care." Ariana thought about the brave little fox cub. It knew there was something wrong with the water and had gotten them to follow it. "The others are right—we have to find out what's going on."

She shrugged off her backpack and, dropping to her hands and knees, crawled to the cliff edge. She flattened her stomach to the ground, held tight to the rocky edge, and peered over it. She could see her friends at the bottom, searching for clues. A few yards below her, a slow stream

of water was trickling from the hole in the rocks. But what was that noise? From the cave came a dull, rumbling roar. It sounded as if there was a massive river flowing beneath her. Where was it going if it wasn't flowing out of the opening?

Ariana crawled back to Whisper. "I need to look in the cave," she told him.

Whisper's ears flickered, and he looked worried. "That sounds dangerous," he said. "You'll have to climb down the cliff."

"I'll be okay. I brought a flashlight and a rope with me, and it's not far down." Ariana started unpacking her

backpack. Pulling out the rope, she tied one end around her waist, making sure the knot was secure. Then she wrapped the other end around an outcrop of rock and tied it tight. She took out the flashlight and put it into her pocket. "Wait here. If I need help, I'll shout for you. Hold on to the rope in case it comes off the rock I've tied it to!"

Whisper nodded. "I will."

Ariana took a deep breath. She really didn't want to climb over the edge of the cliff and go into the dark, mysterious cave, but she knew she had to. She was going to be a guardian one day, and that meant she had to protect Unicorn Island and stop anyone who wanted to harm it—or the creatures who lived there.

"You can do this, Ariana," said Whisper as if reading her thoughts. He nuzzled her hair. "I know you can."

As he breathed warmly on her cheek, her courage rose. Dropping to her hands and knees, she crawled to the edge, and trying not to look at the drop below, she turned around and lowered herself over it. Using the rocks that jutted out for handholds and footholds, she inched her way down the cliff toward the opening, her nails breaking on the rocks, her clothes getting streaked with even more dirt.

Suddenly she heard a shout from below. "Look at Ariana!" It was Matilda. Ariana didn't dare look down, but whinnies and shouts rose to her ears.

"Ariana! What are you doing?" Violet shrieked.

"Be careful!" cried Freya.

"Oh, wow, Ariana!" That was Rosa. She sounded very impressed.

Ariana forced herself to block out their voices and concentrate on what she was doing. If she

slipped, she had no idea if the rope would hold her weight.

Just a little bit farther, she told herself firmly. *Keep going.*

She was level with the cave entrance now. Gripping the edges of the cave, she swung her feet inside. She heard her friends gasp as her feet hit the rocky floor and she wriggled into the dark hole. *Yes! She'd made it!*

She was standing on solid ground inside the cave, a fine spray of water soaking into her hair and clothes. The rumbling and roaring were even louder here. Pulling her flashlight out, she gasped. It was the strangest thing she had ever seen. A large river was flowing through the cave, straight

93

toward the cave entrance and toward her, but for some reason, about three yards from her feet, the river just stopped and seemed to vanish into thin air. Why? The beam of her flashlight caught on ten blue pearls that were laid out in a line on the rocky floor, just where the river vanished. Ariana edged closer. The pearls sparkled in the light. She had seen something like them before. . . .

Rain seeds! They were magical seeds, Ariana remembered. Not only could they make rain, but when they were placed near a body of water, a spell could be put on them to make that water vanish and reappear somewhere else. Her dad had shown her a picture of them last year and told her that the previous head teacher of Unicorn Academy—Ms. Primrose—had used them to try to shut the academy down by causing Sparkle Lake to flood. Someone must be using them here

to transport the magic river somewhere else—maybe so they could use its magic power!

Right now, Ariana knew she didn't have time to think about who might do such a thing or why. She had to remove the seeds. But how? If she picked them up, the river would start flowing again, and she'd be swept out of the cave in the torrent of water. It was a steep drop, and she probably wouldn't survive. No, there had to be a safer way to move the seeds. In her head, Ariana ran through the items in her backpack. A smile spread across her face. Oh yes, she might have just the thing she needed!

CHAPTER 9

A few minutes later, Ariana was back outside the cave, balancing on the rocky footholds and clinging on with one hand. In the other, she held the collapsible fishing net she'd packed. She'd extended the pole to its limit, and it was now several yards long.

"What are you doing?" Rosa shouted.

"Ariana, have you gone nuts?" yelled Matilda. "You can't fish up there!"

Ariana ignored them. "Whisper! Are you holding tightly?" she shouted up the cliff.

"Yes!" Whisper whinnied. "When are you coming back?"

"In a moment—I hope. But first I have to do this. Hold tight for me!" Taking a deep breath and trusting Whisper with her whole heart, she let go of the handhold and swung the net inside the cave. She swiped it along the blue rain seeds, scooping them up. As she pulled the net back, the river came crashing through the opening, its spray drenching her from head to toe as it fell in a glittering, sparkling sheet into the pool below.

"Oh no!" gasped Ariana when she heard her friends' screams of surprise as the water cascaded down. Their screams turned into shrieks of delight as they started splashing around in the rapidly filling pool with their unicorns.

"The river's flowing again!" cried Rosa.

"The waterfall is back!" shouted Freya.

Feeling a rush of relief, Ariana folded up the net, put the rain seeds in her pocket, and started to climb back up the cliff.

By the time she reached Whisper, she was shaking with relief and could barely untie the rope from around her waist. She leaned against him and he nuzzled her, his breath drying her damp skin. "What happened? Are you okay?" he demanded.

"Yes, I'm fine," she said, hugging him. She quickly told him what had happened.

"You're so brave!" he told her, his eyes round with awe. "You saved the waterfall and made it flow again!"

Ariana smiled. "Come on, let's go tell the others," she said.

When Whisper and Ariana reached the pool, it had filled completely. A stream was flowing away from it again, carrying the clean magic water off through the trees for all the animals in the woods to drink.

"Okay, you have some serious explaining to do!"

said Rosa as the girls and their unicorns waded out to greet Ariana and Whisper. "What do you think you were doing climbing down a cliff, swinging from a rope, disappearing into a cave . . . ?"

"It was nothing," said Ariana modestly.

"She was amazing," said Whisper proudly. He told the others what Ariana had done.

"Rain seeds," breathed Freya. "I've heard about them."

Ariana pulled the bright blue seeds out of her pocket. "They were what was causing all the problems. Someone must have wanted to send the river somewhere else."

"But why?" said Violet.

"To use its magic in some way, I guess," suggested Freya. "I wonder who it was."

"We'll have to tell the teachers about this, but . . . wow!" Rosa shook her head. "You saved the day, Ariana."

"With a fishing net!" said Matilda, her eyes wide.

"I told you all the things I had might come in handy!" said Ariana.

"I'm really sorry I teased you for having such a big backpack now!" Matilda said.

"Me too," said Rosa. "It was really smart of you."

Ariana grinned. "Just call me Little Miss Organized."

"You're brilliant! No one is ever allowed to tease you for being organized again!" Rosa declared. The unicorns whinnied in agreement.

Ariana felt as if she was glowing inside. "That's okay. I don't mind being teased." She meant it. As she looked around at her friends' happy faces, she suddenly realized that, for the first time, she really felt part of the dorm—part of a team.

Violet hugged her. "Oh, sorry," she said as she

looked at the mud she'd just left on Ariana. She giggled happily. "Oh dear, I guess we all look like mud monsters today!"

Crystal plunged into the pool. "I'm going to get clean!" she said. "Who's going to join me?"

With a chorus of delighted whinnies, the other unicorns cantered after her.

"Come on in, Ariana!" called Whisper as he splashed into the water. "The water's lovely and clean now!"

Ariana decided she was so wet already she might as well join in. Whisper stamped his hooves, splashing her with multicolored water. It was so cold it made her gasp, but it was also crystal clear and washed all the mud away. She spun around in it, feeling tingly with happiness.

"See, it's not so bad being outdoors, is it?" asked Whisper.

"No, it's not," said Ariana, hugging him.

"Thanks for making me realize that."

"Can we do more outdoorsy things from now on?" asked Whisper eagerly.

"Definitely!" said Ariana.

"Though braiding and grooming are okay too." Whisper nuzzled her. "I want us both to do things we like and be happy."

"I am happy because you make me very happy," Ariana said, kissing him on the nose. "You're the best unicorn in the world!"

"Water fight!" shrieked Rosa, splashing water around.

Everyone joined in, squealing with laughter.

"Girls!" A sharp voice broke through the air. "What on earth is going on?"

They all stopped and looked

around. Ms. Rivers was on the bank, sitting astride her unicorn, Lady.

"You're supposed to be conducting a survey of animals on the outskirts of the woods, not playing games in the middle. I realized you were missing and have been very worried. Come out and explain yourselves at once!" she said.

"We're sorry, Ms. Rivers, but please don't be mad. We think we have figured out what's been going on, and Ariana's fixed it," Rosa explained as everyone waded out of the pool.

"What do you mean?" Ms. Rivers's stern look faded. "No, first, let's get you all dry, and then you can explain." She touched Lady's neck. The unicorn shook her mane, sparkles flew into the air, and a second later the girls felt a warm breeze swirling around them, drying their skin and clothes and leaving them toasty warm. "That's better," said Ms. Rivers. "Thank you, Lady."

Lady gave a soft snort and nuzzled her leg.

"Now tell me what's been going on," the teacher said.

The girls explained what had been happening—the angry animals, the sludgy pool, the river that had been disappearing because of rain seeds.

"Ariana got the rain seeds—" said Rosa.

"With a fishing net," Matilda added helpfully.

"And now the waterfall is flowing again," said Freya, gesturing to the Verdant Falls. "Look!"

"Ariana was amazing," said Violet.

"Well, well, well," said Ms. Rivers, shaking her head. "This is very worrying. I must tell Ms. Nettles about it as soon as we get back." Her face broke into a rare smile. "Well done, everyone. You've solved the mystery. The animals must have been leaving the woods because the pool was drying up. Now hopefully all will be well again."

"Though we need to find out who was responsible," said Rosa.

"Indeed," said Ms. Rivers. "But now let's leave the woodland animals in peace and go back to the school—I imagine you must all be very hungry. I think hot baths and a large supper are called for."

"Ariana! Your hair!" Violet said suddenly. "You've bonded with Whisper!"

Ariana dipped her head and saw that one of her braids had turned the same pink and purple colors as Whisper's mane. Happiness rushed through her, and she ran to where Whisper was standing with the other unicorns. Flinging her arms around him, she gasped, "We've bonded, Whisper!"

Whisper nuzzled her neck. "I always knew we would."

Ariana felt like she was going to burst with delight. Turning around, she saw all her friends

beaming. *My friends,* she thought happily. *All of them.*

"I'm so glad you came to Unicorn Academy, and we were paired together," said Whisper, nudging her shoulder.

"Me too," she said, laughing and hugging him again. "Now let's go back to school and have even more fun!"

PERSONALITY QUIZ

What power would YOUR unicorn have?
Take this quiz to find out!

As soon as I arrive at Unicorn Academy, I . . .

A) Get to know everyone in my dorm
B) Make sure my dorm is as clean and sparkly as possible
C) Unpack pictures of my family so I can look at them when I'm missing home
D) Explore the grounds— I want to see everything!
E) Challenge everyone to a race around the lake

My favorite thing to do with my unicorn is . . .

A) Galloping as fast as we can around Unicorn Island
B) Braiding their mane with sparkly ribbons
C) Exploring Unicorn Island and learning how to protect the environment together
D) Going on adventures!
E) Leaping as high as we can over jumps

My favorite class at Unicorn Academy is . . .

A) Geography and Culture of Unicorn Island
B) Care of Unicorns
C) Nature Studies
D) I would rather be on an adventure!
E) Cross-country

My friends would describe me as . . .

A) Fun
B) Animal obsessed
C) Caring
D) Daring
E) Competitive

The best place to hang out at Unicorn Academy is . . .

A) The grounds–where there's so much to explore
B) The stables–where I can groom my unicorn
C) The garden–so I can look after all the plants
D) The woods–where we can go on lots of long rides
E) The library–so I can learn as much about my unicorn as possible

If you answered . . .

Mostly As

Your unicorn would have speed magic! They can gallop so fast it feels like flying.

Mostly Bs

Your unicorn would have soothing magic. They can calm animals and people and help them become friends.

Mostly Cs

Your unicorn would have healing magic! They can take away aches and pains.

Mostly Ds

Your unicorn would have light magic! They can create light and rainbow bridges.

Mostly Es

Your unicorn would have flying magic! They can soar high above the others.

READ MORE ABOUT

UNICORN ACADEMY

UNICORN ACADEMY
Layla and Dancer

JULIE SYKES ★ illustrated by LUCY TRUMAN

UNICORN ACADEMY
Olivia and Snowflake

JULIE SYKES ★ illustrated by LUCY TRUMAN

UNICORN ACADEMY
Rosa and Crystal

JULIE SYKES ★ illustrated by LUCY TRUMAN

UNICORN ACADEMY
Ariana and Whisper

JULIE SYKES ★ illustrated by LUCY TRUMAN

Meet your newest feline friends!

Purrmaids
The Scaredy Cat

1

Sudipta Bardhan-Quallen

rhcbooks.com RHCB

New friends. New adventures.
Find a new series ... just for you!

For ballerina and fairy and vampire lovers

For adventurers

For unicorn lovers

For dog lovers

For mermaid and cat lovers

For sports fans

rhcbooks.com